To Elizabeth my life and my love!   -S.T.

To Blue and Noah who make every day like
Christmas Morning. I♡U!   -Daddy

Rudolf the Red Nose Rocket

One cold winter night Santa took the Great List,
checking the names twice so no one was missed.

The elves were fishing through holes in the lake,
Mrs. Claus in the kitchen making cookies to bake.

The elves and reindeer began such a clatter,
Santa threw open the door shouting, "What is the matter?"

A streak in the sky, a glaring bright glow,
shed the luster of daylight to objects in snow.

Suddenly a blast knocked Santa flat on his back,
as a heat flash melted the workshop snow pack.

Then, what to his wondering eye should appear,
but a crash landing spaceship with alien in headgear!

The little alien crawled out, hit the ground with a clunk,
aimed a kick at the hull, and yelled out "Space Junk!"

She was dressed all in plastic, and covered in muck
from her spaceship splashing up mud where it struck.

The space elf was pretty, six fingers and toes,
and strange green spots around her mouth and her nose.

She chunked off her helmet so lively and quick,
then shook out her hair- pink, wild, and thick.

Santa greeted her warmly, "Welcome my friend!
You must be a life form from a far distant land."

"Pinky's the name," she replied shaking and shivering.
"I'm freezing!" she said, her lips quaking and quivering.

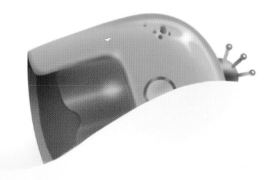

"My name is Santa, you're at the North Pole.
Come in and dry off before you catch cold!"

Santa grabbed her hand and gave it a shake.
It felt clammy and sticky like old shake and bake.

"Come in, and sit down, we will all want to talk.
We were told long ago about far flung elf flocks."

"Sit by the fire and warm yourself up-
I'll grab us some hot chocolate milk in a cup."

Mrs. Claus came from the kitchen and saw Pinky's spots,
saying, "Now, hold still dear, let me check if you're hot!"

She thought Pinky was local, another Elf from the wood;
she didn't realize the alien was from a space neighborhood.

"You feel like wet seafood, maybe scallops or clams,
or that gelatin stuff I scrape off the spam."

"You don't feel right for an elf! How are your lungs?"
Your color's not right. Now, stick out your tongue!"

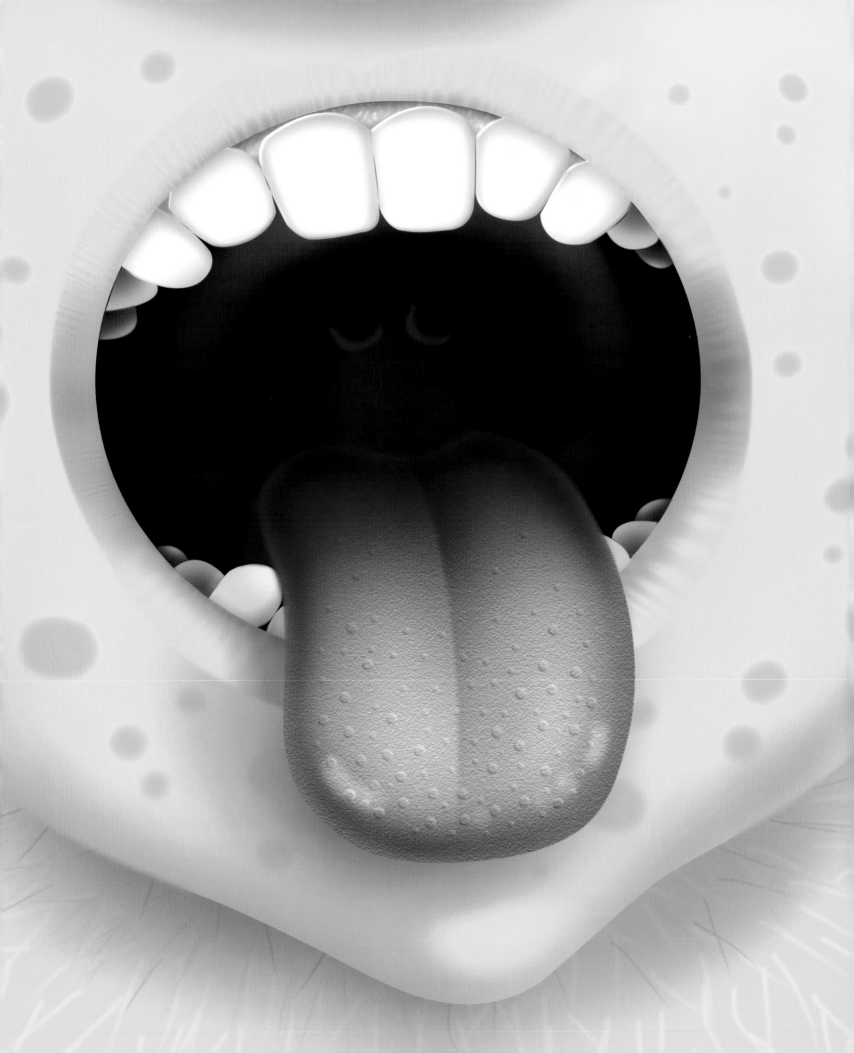

Entering the workshop, Pinky was struck with such awe,
a golden glow filled everything that she saw.

The elves were all busy fixing ribbons to be tied
on presents for children for the great Christmas ride.

"This place is so busy and pulsing with light,
what is it that makes it so joyful and bright?"

"What is this place where you hammer and tap?
Why do you make toys like this one and that?"

Oh dear," she squinted, "You should be in bed.
It might be my vision, but I see spots on your head."

"Find your glasses," said Santa, "you are mistaken, my dear!
Pinky's no elf! She's a space visitor here."

"Oh, where do you come from? What's it like up in space?
Are the stars there all different? Is it a far away place?"

"Please tell us stories! We'll gather the elves all around.
Got any about monsters or hairy space hounds?"

"What is this strangeness I feel in the air,
this pulsing, this feeling, this desire to share?"

"It's a gift of the Life that we serve at the shop.
We're getting ready for Christmas and all the sleigh stops!"

"Christmas? What's Christmas?" Pinky was puzzled.
Suddenly all sounds of working were muzzled.

The hammers stopped tapping, it was silent as death.
No sound was heard, not even a breath.

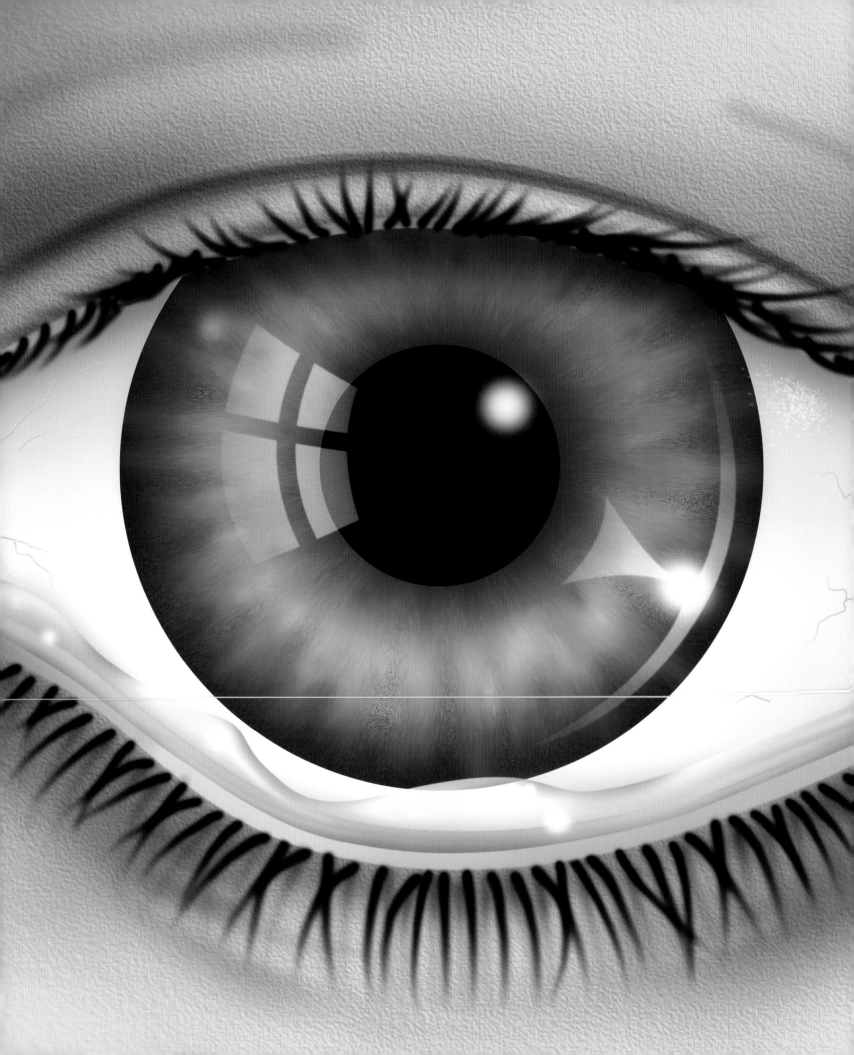

"Our space kin don't know about Christmas?" they cried,
tears forming quickly in each elfin eye.

"Let me tell you about Christmas," Santa said with a grin,
"Earth was visited by Jesus who had love for all men."

"He first came to us announced by a star,
elves dressed as kings brought him gifts from afar."

"At the end of his time on the earth with the men,
he came for a visit with the elves and their kin."

"He taught us to love as he visited each elf
and when he left us he left part of himself."

"It is that joyful presence you feel in the air,
it teaches us love, and helps us to share."

"So each year at Christmas to honor his birth,
we bring presents to children living on earth."

"He taught us that life can be endless you see,
the very presence of love lives in you and in me."

"For love is perfect- the greatest of things,
flowing from life's endless internal spring."

"At Christmas, we pack presents, hitch sleigh and reindeer,
telling the gift of his life and spreading good cheer."

"I must tell others," said Pinky, "on the planets up there,
of this message of love and this feeling you share!"

"I've got to get ready and take this message of hope
to new worlds in space! Oh fudge, My rocket is broke!"

Pinky heard Santa mutter, "I'd like to see stars!
If we built a rocket I could fly by and see Mars."

The elves went to work finding the parts,
a task that was loved by each elf at heart.

They found an old 454 with cam overhead,
built an airtight body, painted the nose candy red.

Four barrel ignition with four on the floor,
plenty of room on the inside to store presents galore!

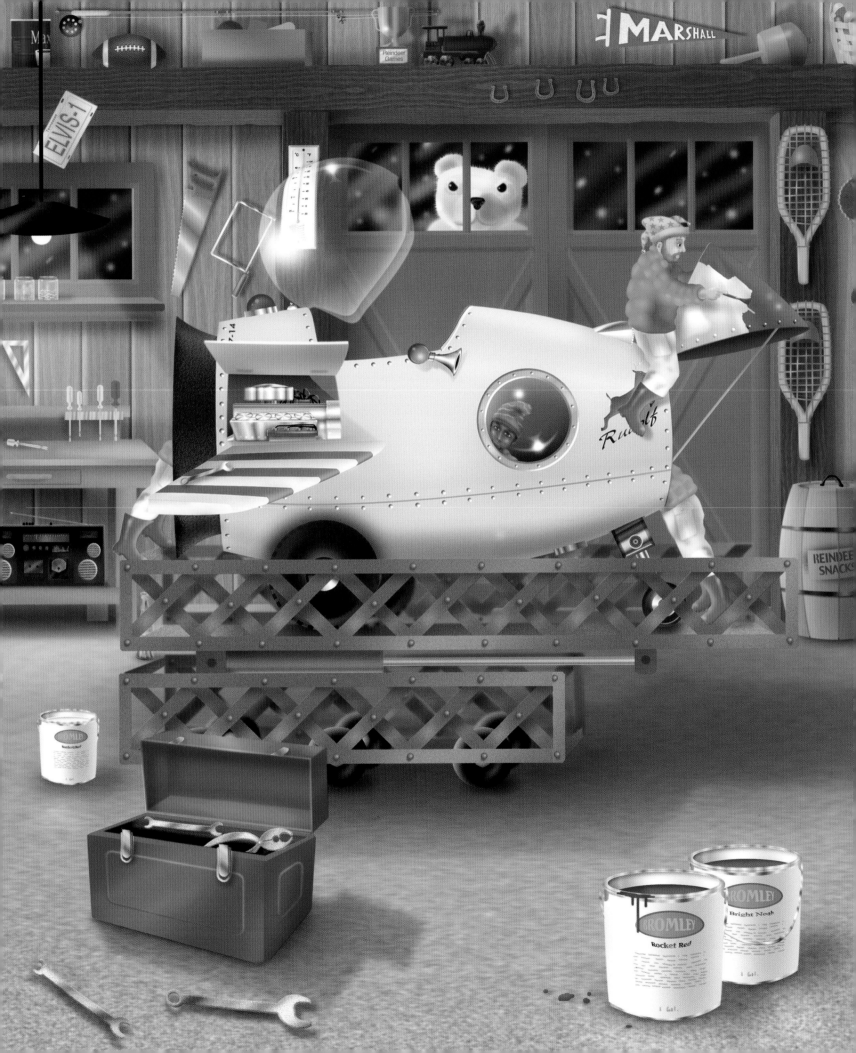

When the rocket was ready Santa declared amid cheers,
"This spaceship is named for Rudolph Reindeer!"

"Rudolf will guide us again as he did once before,
as we travel past stars far from earth's shore."

"Pinky!" Santa called, "We have to hurry and go.
I have to get back for the big Christmas show!"

Mrs. Claus had sewed Santa a jacket and cap,
Elf Space Control checked rockets and flaps.

Soon the rocket was ready, red nose toward the sky,
Santa and Pinky gathered the elves for goodbye.

Mrs. Claus wrapped a scarf around Pinky's cold neck.
Hugging Santa, she gave his cheek a quick peck.

Off for the stars they blasted that night,
but before the rocket could pass beyond sight,

The elves could hear Pinky exclaim with delight,
"Merry Christmas to all Life Forms on Rudolph's first flight!"

THE END

Steve Tiller was delivered as an early Christmas present. It was so long ago not even his mother is sure of the exact year. He came loosely wrapped. The Angels were singing, kind of humming actually. His parents were ecstatic. His brother and sister were less than thrilled. That state of affairs hasn't changed much after all these years. The family still gives him mixed reviews, he can still hear the low hum of the Angels, and his wrapping is still loose.

Daddy and Computer Folk Artist **Robert Cremeans** was born barefoot in almost heaven West Virginia. Where it is so beautiful that doing art just comes natural. He studied business at Sheperd College, science at Marshall University and graduated with a B.F.A. from Columbus College of Art and Design. He now lives in Atlanta, Georgia with his beautiful children Blue and Noah.